This book is for:

Love,

Copyright © 2022 Patricia Eckerman Ambas

No part of this publication may be reproduced, distributed, or transmitted in any form or by any means, including photocopying, recording, or other electronic or mechanical methods, without prior written permission of the publisher, except in the case of brief quotations embodied in reviews and certain other non-commercial uses permitted by copyright law.
Designed by Olga Pinto

ISBN 978-1-958497-01-2

This book is dedicated to Reginald, my second "baby package"
and inventor of this game. – Patricia

To Nour, my sweet little brother. – Amira

Visit *ICantWaitToLoveYouForever.com* for fun ideas to use with this story!

I can't wait to Love You Forever

WRITTEN BY
Patricia Eckerman Ambas

iLLUSTRATED BY
Amira Daaboul

"DING DONG! A package for my mommy!"
Benjamin announced.

His mom peered around the corner. A suspicious little lump of a blanket sat in the middle of the living room floor.

Mommy sashayed towards it, tapping her chin.

"I wonder what it could be.
I wasn't expecting a package!"

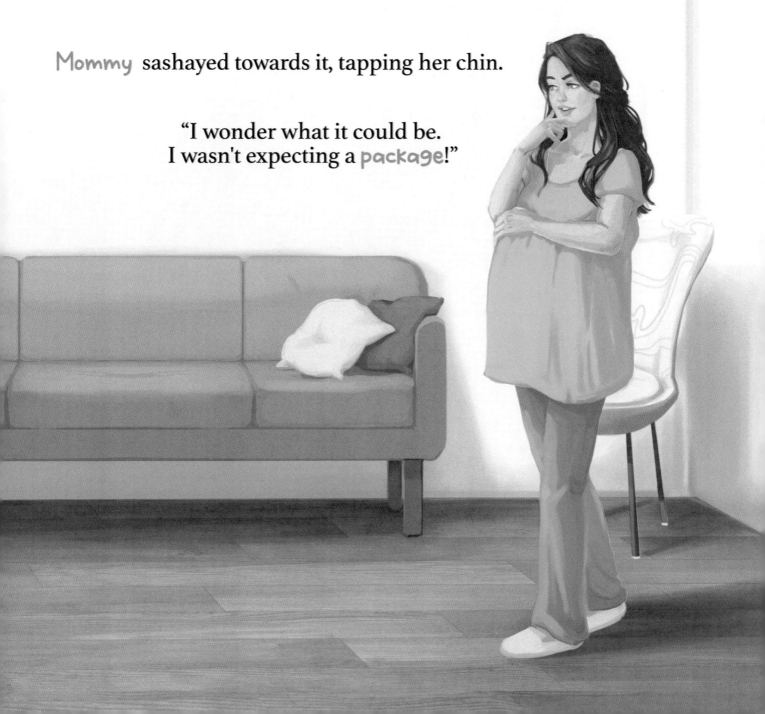

"Criiiiict. Criiiiict," she said,
pretending to break the seal on the imaginary box.

Mommy gently pulled back
Benjamin's
lovie blanket and gasped
when she uncovered his face.

"Oh! It's a sweet baby!
I must be the luckiest Mommy in the world!
I can't wait to love you forever, sweet baby,"

she crooned to Benjamin
and picked him up,
cradling her son like a baby.

But this baby's legs hung far over Mommy's arms,
and his head came up high above her shoulder.

Still, she carried him and sat down with him
on her lap.

"Are you my sweet baby?" she asked.

Benjamin made his eyes big and his mouth tiny.
Then he nodded back at her.

"And will you be my sweet child when you are a
big boy, too?"
He nodded again.

"Goo goo gah gah,"
he announced in a loud voice and squirmed to get down.

Benjamin crawled away like a baby
on his hands and knees.

Mommy smiled after him and stood up,
placing a hand on her round tummy.

"DING DONG! A package for my mommy!"

"I wonder what it could be. I wasn't expecting a `package`," she said.

A giggle escaped from the upside-down laundry basket.

She bent over it. "Criiiiict. Criiiiict," she said,
pulling back imaginary flaps on the box.

"What is this?"
her shocked voice asked as she lifted the basket.

Criiiiict
Criiiiict

"Is this a baby?
Oh, it is! I must be the luckiest Mommy in the world!"
she said.

"I can't wait to love you forever,
sweet baby."

She picked him up to cuddle
him close.

"Do you know I love playing Baby Package with you?"
she asked her child with the pretend baby face.

Benjamin blinked back at her.

"Mommy," he finally whispered, "babies can't talk."

"Yes, you're right.
I just keep hoping that one of these packages will have a
sweet BIG boy in it," she whispered back.

He baby-blinked at her again.

"I love babies, but I also love big boys,"
she said, patting him and setting him on the floor.

"Coooo, coooo,"
was Benjamin's pretend baby response.

"DING DONG! A package for my mommy!"

Benjamin later called, running into his bedroom.

Mommy turned off the bathroom light and stopped at his doorway.

"A package?" she asked.

"For me?"

She watched his shape move under the blanket.

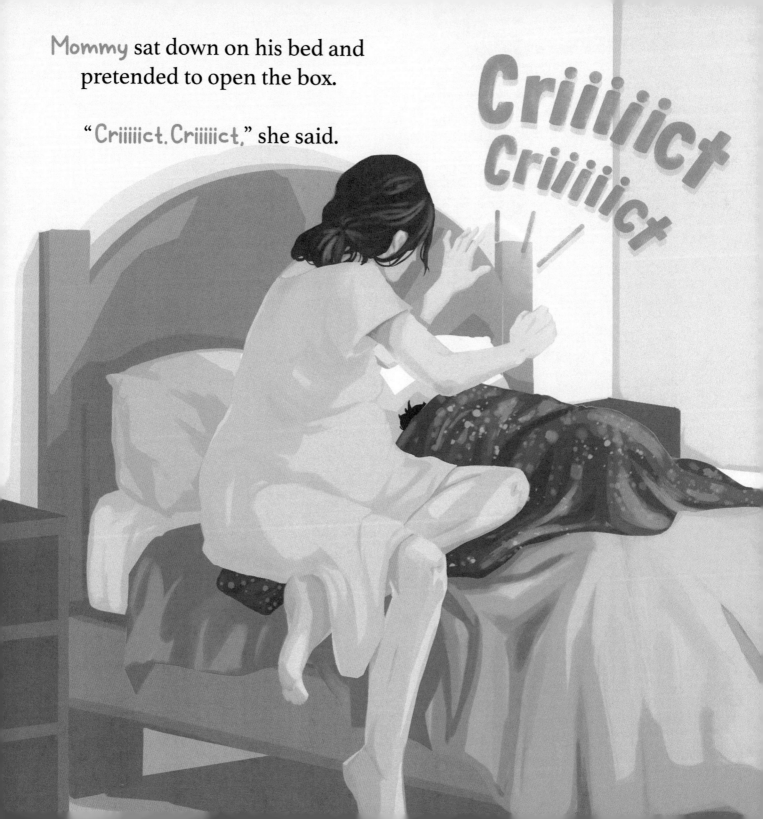

Then she reached down and tugged his blanket until his
tightly closed eyes were in view.

"Oh! It's a sleepy baby!
I must be the luckiest Mommy in the world!

I can't wait to love you forever, sweet baby,"
she said, kissing his face until he giggled.

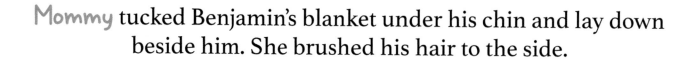

Mommy tucked Benjamin's blanket under his chin and lay down beside him. She brushed his hair to the side.

"Do you have any questions about the baby coming?" she asked. When he didn't respond, she continued, "It will be fun to have a baby in our house. You are going to be such a great big brother.

I can't wait for you to teach the baby all of your games."

"The baby can play games with me?" Benjamin asked.

"Well, not right away. When the baby first comes, we will be very gentle and let them sleep a lot so that they can grow," Mommy explained.

"And then when they grow bigger, you can play games with him or her!" she added.

Benjamin smiled, snuggling deeper into his bed.

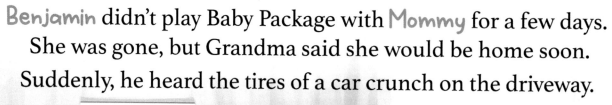

Benjamin didn't play Baby Package with Mommy for a few days.
She was gone, but Grandma said she would be home soon.
Suddenly, he heard the tires of a car crunch on the driveway.

Running to the window, Benjamin
saw Mommy and Daddy getting out.

He ran to get his lovie and put it over himself,
crouching into a tiny package.

He waited for the right moment. Before he could say ding dong,
he heard his Mommy's voice call out,

"DING DONG! A package for my Benjamin!"
Benjamin peeked his head out.

He heard it again.
"DING DONG! A package for
my Benjamin!"

DING
DONG

He whipped off his lovie and ran to the kitchen.
Mommy and Daddy stood there smiling at him.

By their feet was something
round covered with a blanket.

As he came nearer,
they bent down.
Mommy quietly
urged him,
"Go ahead. Open it."

"Criiiiict. Criiiiict," he said as he pretended to open the box.

He hesitantly lifted the edge of the blanket until he could see inside.

"It's a baby!" he said.

"Yes, it's a sweet baby.
You must be the luckiest brother in the world!
I can't wait for you to love each other forever," she said softly.

Benjamin stared at that
little baby face.
Big eyes looking at him.
A tiny mouth. It really
was a baby package!

The next day, "DING DONG! A package for my Mommy!"
sang Benjamin.

Mommy turned towards Benjamin's voice and
was surprised to see him standing right behind her.
He reached out to take her hand.
"Come on! I'll show you your package!" he said.

He pulled her along, right to the corner where
Baby lay in the bassinet
with their eyes closed.

"Shhhhh," he said,
"Baby is sleeping. Open it quietly."

Benjamin's face beamed up at Mommy.

She reached down to take off the invisible packaging.
In a hushed voice, she said, "Criiiiict. Criiiiict.

"Oh! It's a sweet baby!
I must be the luckiest Mommy in the world to
have a baby AND a big boy!

I can't wait to love you both forever,"
she whispered as she pulled Benjamin against her.

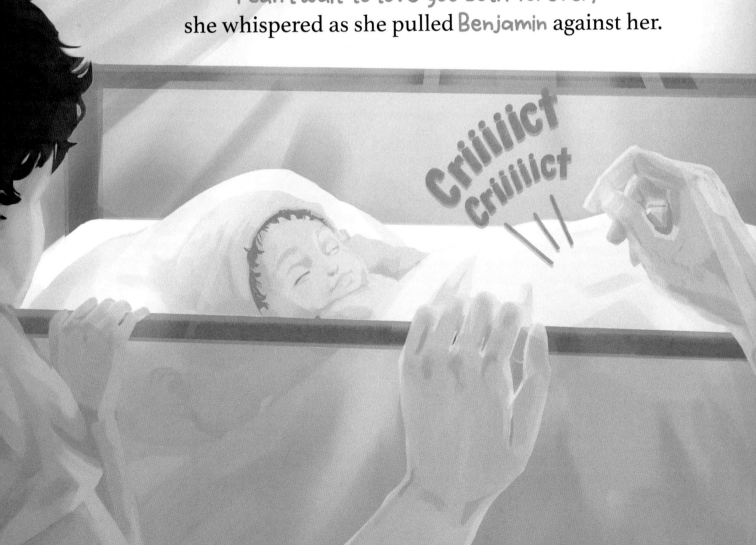

Benjamin reached out and touched his fingertips to Baby's tummy.

"I can't wait to love you forever."

The End

Do you want to color the same picture as Benjamin?
Ask your adult to visit: *ICantWaitToLoveYouForever.com* to download this coloring page.
Color it for fun or to welcome your own sweet baby!

Please share your completed pictures with the author
at *PatriciaEckermanAmbas.com* or tag her on social media *@PatriciaEckermanAmbas*
she can't wait to love your art!

Patricia Eckerman Ambas

As a mom of three and Auntie/Tita to many, Patricia has seen the joy new babies bring into families and the powerful connection siblings have with each other.

Before her third baby was born,
Baby Package was created and played constantly!
Once the baby arrived, her son still loved to play Baby Package!

She hopes this book is a fun way to introduce
a new game into your home.
As a teacher, she enjoys the concept of using real life scenes
along with playful imagination to warm up siblings to the idea of a baby's arrival.

Follow along at @PatriciaEckermanAmbas on social media
or at PatriciaEckermanAmbas.com
for upcoming books and family fun!

Amira Daaboul

Amira is a curious human driven to discover
the limitless art world.

She started doodling on school books, walls and bed
up until she pursued her ambition of becoming a
professional fine artist.

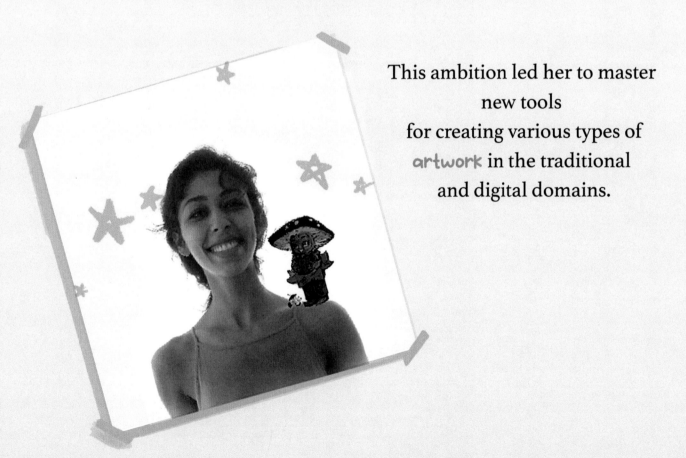

This ambition led her to master
new tools
for creating various types of
artwork in the traditional
and digital domains.

Made in the USA
Las Vegas, NV
16 October 2023

79227571R00021